How Much WOOD Could a Woodchuck Chuck?

Other Adlerman books

Africa Calling, Nighttime Falling
Rub a Dub Dub
Rock-a-bye Baby
Songs for America's Children
How Much Wood Could a Woodchuck Chuck?
Oh No, Domino!
Mommy's Having a Watermelon

by Kin Eagle *(Danny and Kim's pen name)*
(illustrated by Roby Gilbert)

It's Raining, It's Pouring
Hey, Diddle Diddle
Humpty Dumpty

Adlerman music

One Size Fits All
Listen UP!
...and a Happy New Year

How Much WOOD Could a Woodchuck Chuck?

The Kids at Our House

by **Danny Adlerman**

illustrated by Kim Adlerman • Roby Gilbert

Megan Halsey • Ryan Hipp • Kevin Kammeraad

Jill Kastner • Judy Love • Michael Paraskevas

Lena Shiffman • Javaka Steptoe

Joel Tanis • Liza Woodruff

music by **Jim Babjak**

A note to parents and teachers

Hello, parents and teachers!

We hope you have enjoyed this book as much as your child or children have. We made it for you, too! You must be careful, though: The book is so infectiously catchy in so many ways, your lives may be indelibly altered by it. You may be singing the song forevermore; you could be listening to retellings of the lyric for the rest of your life. You or your child may even want to cut out pictures from the book to hang on your walls. You'd then have to buy another one to keep for your collection. We can't be held responsible for that. We're sure you understand!

However, there are also some keen and practical ways this package can be used not only to enhance story time but as a learning tool, too. The rhymes are made out of either compound words (such as woodchuck and chuck wood) or inverse descriptives (for example, strawberry and bury straw). One or two were put in purely for fun, which we sometimes forget is a good thing! In the back of the book you will find a CD that has the song, rendered in two ways: first, exactly as it first appeared on Danny's album *One Size Fits All*, and second, as an instrumental version, so that you and your child or children can make up rhymes, compound words, and inverse descriptives at home or in the classroom. You will also find the music to the first two phrases printed in the book, complete with lyrics, so that you can sing it with or without the CD. See how thoughtful we are?

We hope you love this book and have as much fun with it as all of us have had...and we also hope you use it as a fun educational tool. We believe the more fun learning is, the easier it is to learn!

Thanks again, and peace!

● ●

Copyright ©2006 by Danny Adlerman
Illustrations ©2006 by *The Kids at Our House*
Lyrics and music ©2001 by Danny Adlerman and Jim Babjak

The Kids at Our House
47 Stoneham Place
Metuchen, NJ 08840
www.dannyandkim.com
info@dannyandkim.com

Library of Congress Cataloging-in-Publication Data available on request

ISBN-13: 978-09705773-4-4 (hc)
ISBN-13: 978-09705773-5-1 (sc)

10 9 8 7 6 5 4 3 (hc)   10 9 8 7 6 5 4 3 2 (sc)

The display type was set in Humanist 521 Bold.
The text type was set in Goudy Old Style Bold.
Manufactured in China by Jade Productions, December 2013
Book production and design by *The Kids at Our House*

Yo Josh, my dude,
How much dew could a doodad add if a doodad could add, dude?
I love you.
Your dude, Dad.

How much wood could a woodchuck chuck
if a woodchuck could chuck wood?

As much wood as a woodchuck could
if a woodchuck could chuck wood!

How much butter could a buttercup cup
if a buttercup could cup butter?

As much butter as a buttercup could
if a buttercup could cup butter!

How much fruit could a fruit bat bat
if a fruit bat could bat fruit?

As much fruit as a fruit bat could
if a fruit bat could bat fruit!

How much straw could a strawberry bury
if a strawberry could bury straw?

As much straw as a strawberry could
if a strawberry could bury straw!

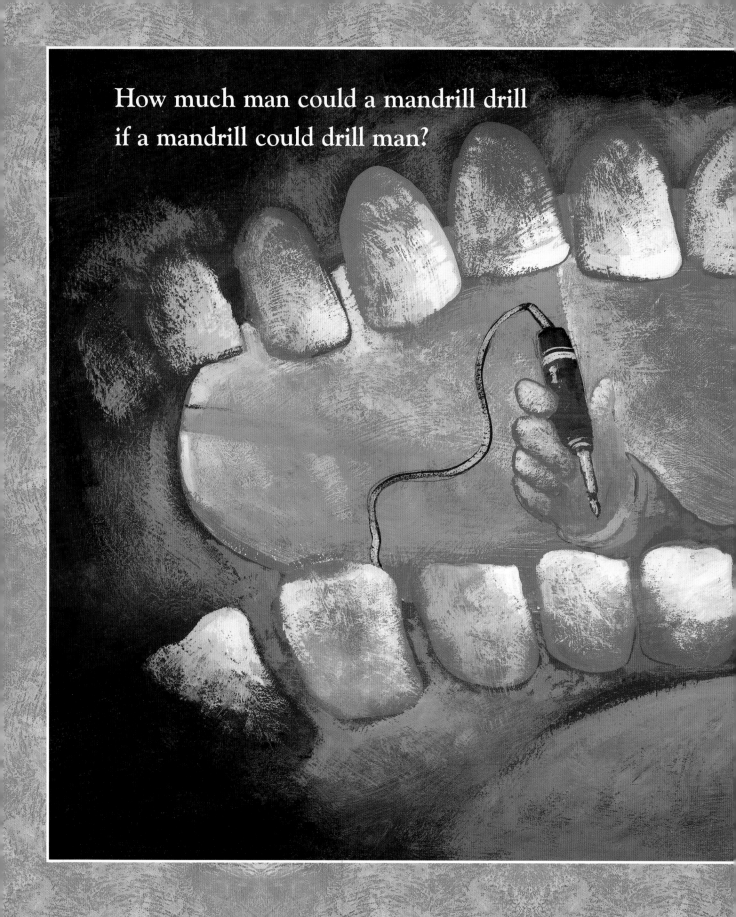

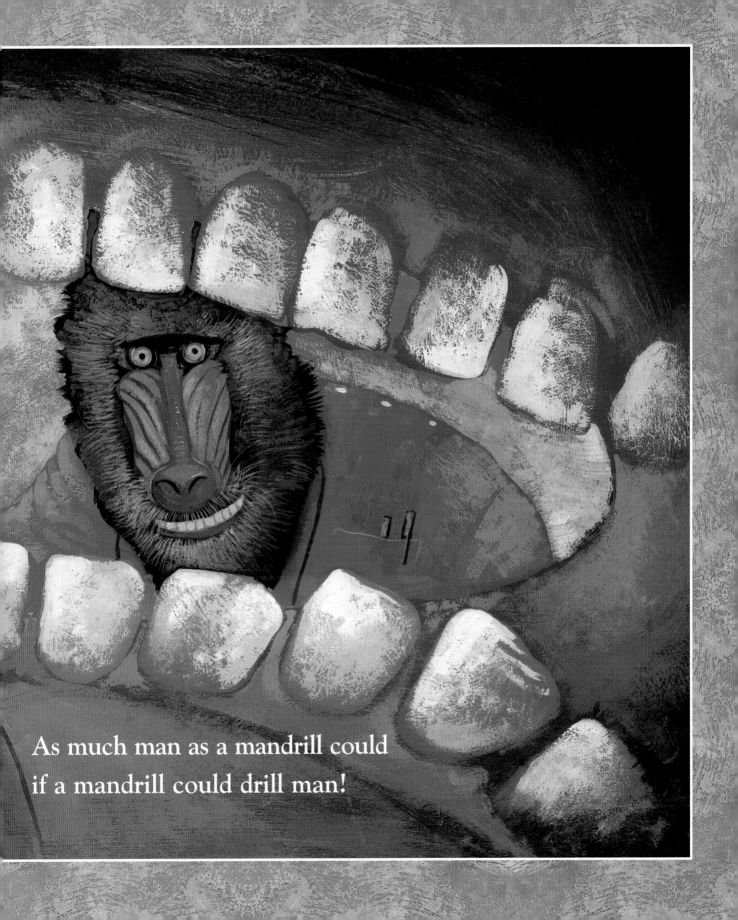

As much man as a mandrill could
if a mandrill could drill man!

How much night could a nightjar jar
if a nightjar could jar night?

As much night as a nightjar could
if a nightjar could jar night!

How much sun could a sun bear bear
if a sun bear could bear sun?

As much sun as a sun bear could
if a sun bear could bear sun!

How much fur could a fur seal seal
if a fur seal could seal

?

As much fur as a fur seal could
if a fur seal could seal fur!

How much chin could a chinchilla chill
if a chinchilla could chill a chin?

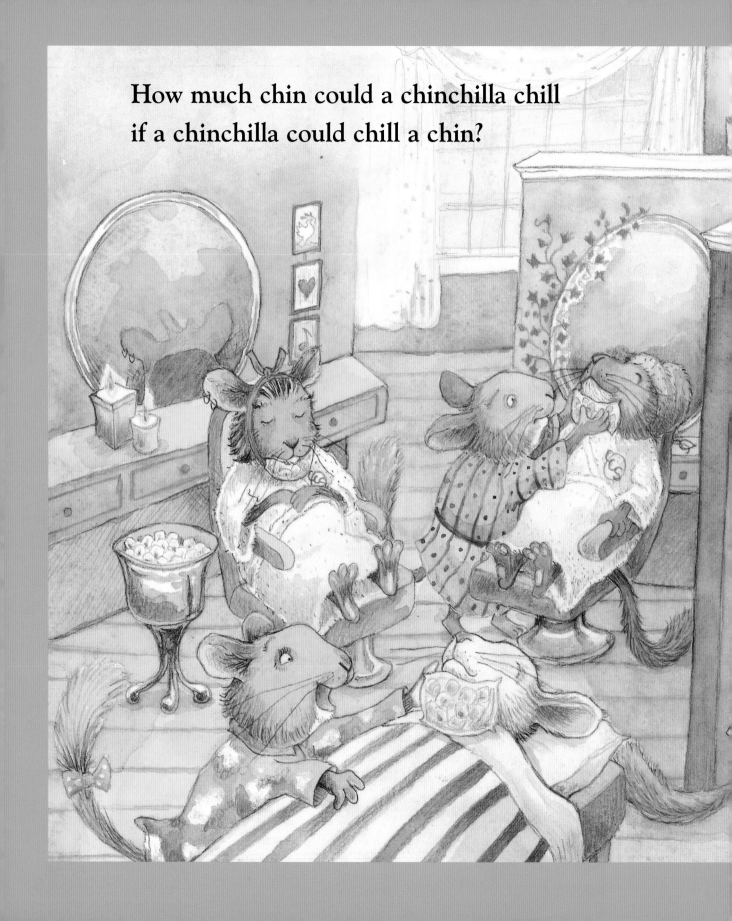

As much chin as a chinchilla could
if a chinchilla could chill a chin!

How much ground could a groundhog hog
if a groundhog could hog ground?

As much ground as a groundhog could
if a groundhog could hog ground!

How much chi could a cheetah tie
if a cheetah could tai chi?

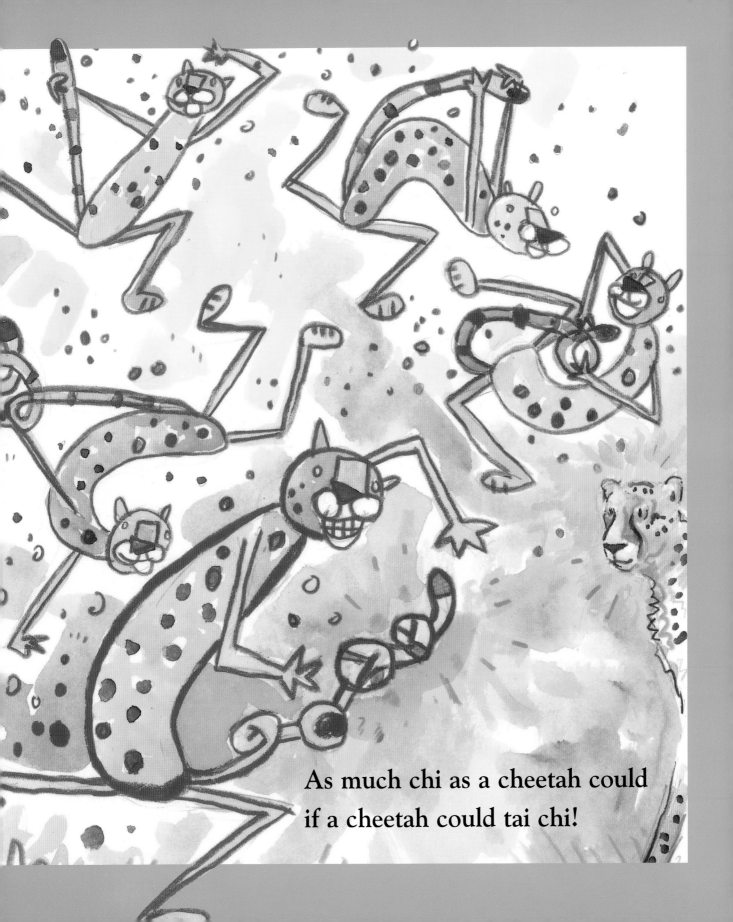

As much chi as a cheetah could
if a cheetah could tai chi!

How much could could a kudu you
if a kudu could you could?

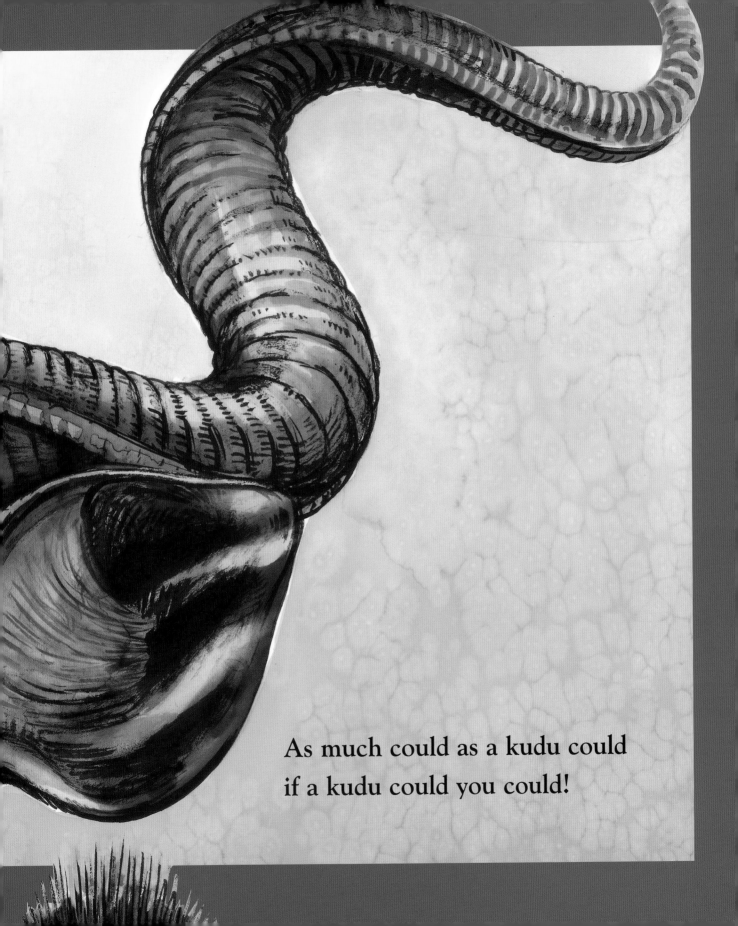

As much could as a kudu could
if a kudu could you could!

Could you?

Meet the artists!

Roby Gilbert was born in New York City. He started working as an animator in 1989 and began illustrating children's books in 1994 with *It's Raining, It's Pouring*, by Kin Eagle. Currently, he teaches animation at the Art Institute of Seattle, illustrates *The Adventures of Ranger Rick* for the National Wildlife Federation, and does various freelance assignments. Roby also performs with a bluegrass ensemble and is a volunteer for TEAM HOPE, offering support to families of missing children. He raises chickens, geese, cats, dogs, and a bunny rabbit in Washington State with his partner, Laura, and their three children.

Jill Kastner was always in trouble as a child for reading under the covers with a flashlight after lights-out. Not content to be alone, she became an illustrator—so a whole new generation of children could get in trouble too. Jill has illustrated more than 25 books, with themes from habitats to pioneers to acrobatic pigs. She finds diverse topics lead to a variety of manuscripts and art styles. Jill's artwork has been exhibited in galleries and art shows nationwide. She finds school visits a welcome change from her desk and easel, and feels that children ask the most insightful questions. They inspire her! Jill lives in Weehawken, New Jersey, with her husband, Tim, and daughters, Carson and Delaney.

Photo by Jennifer Morse

Kevin Kammeraad and his family can be found in Grand Rapids, Michigan, quite possibly working on something related to children's books, music, entertainment, or education. If they're not working, they're probably doing something else. Kevin's books include *The Tomato Collection*, *I Remember*, and *A Curious Glimpse of Michigan* (which he co-wrote with his wife, Stephanie, and co-illustrated with Ryan Hipp). Kevin's father, Steve, and his friend Ryan helped him to create his fruit bat illustration. They sure are nice guys. For more information visit www.tomatocollection.com.

Megan Halsey has illustrated nearly 40 books for children, some of which she also wrote. In addition to her accomplishments in the field of children's books, her editorial work for grown-ups has appeared in major magazines. A former Pratt professor, Megan teaches children's book design and illustration in the Independent Study Master's Degree Program at Marywood University in Scranton, Pennsylvania. Megan lives with her husband, Marty, in Lansdowne, Pennsylvania, where she eats lots of strawberries!

Michael Paraskevas has illustrated for most major magazines over the past 20 years. His illustrations have won him numerous awards from the Society of Illustrators. For the past 12 years he has illustrated his mother Betty's children's books, which include *Junior Kroll*, *Monster Beach*, and *Nibbles O'Hare*. One of their books was recently produced as a popular animated television series, *Maggie and the Ferocious Beast*. The mother-and-son team also write and draw *The Green Monkeys*, a comic strip seen on Long Island and at www.thegreenmonkeys.com. Michael's artwork can be seen at his gallery in Westhampton Beach, New York.

Ryan Hipp is a graphic designer and illustrator of books for kids. He got his start in first grade with a book called *The Penguin Who Froze*, and decided making books was the most important thing in the world. His first book as a grown-up was *A Curious Glimpse of Michigan*, and *How Much Wood Could a Woodchuck Chuck?* is his second book. Ryan lives on Planet Earth in Grand Rapids, Michigan, and also lives on the Internet at www.puppytron.com.

Kim Adlerman has been "arting" for as long as she can remember. She has illustrated *Africa Calling*, *Nighttime Falling*, and *Rock-a-bye Baby* and is the author/illustrator of *Oh No, Domino*. She is also the co-author of several other titles with her husband Danny, including *Mommy's Having a Watermelon*. She found working with so many great artists on *Woodchuck* to be exciting and inspiring. Kim lives very kimberly in New Jersey with her family. They get occasional visits from a woodchuck who is a real veggie muncher. For more information about Kim and her works, check out www.dannyandkim.com.

Javaka Steptoe was born and raised in Brooklyn, New York. A Coretta Scott King Award-winning artist, Javaka is both eclectic and quiet. Although he prefers artistic expression to verbosity, he is unafraid to use his mouth in the consumption of good food—especially grilled salmon. His love of spice is transcendent, however—he enjoys the spice of life that variety offers too! Need more information? Check out www.javaka.com.

Photo by Gary Spector

Liza Woodruff has been illustrating children's books since graduating from the Art Institute of Boston in 1996. She lives and works in northern Vermont with her husband, two children, dog, cats, and sometimes even chickens. When she is not drawing or drowning in laundry, she spends her time wondering just how much wood a Woodruff might ruff.

Lena Shiffman was born in Sweden. She studied at Parsons School of Design and has illustrated many books. Her most recent, *Coralito's Bay*, was written by poet Juan Felipe Herrera. She lives in New Jersey with her husband and daughter.

Joel Tanis isn't very good at tongue twisters. He practices while he draws and paints—what he does most days! Joel has had art shows all over the country, and as far away as Kenya. He has also illustrated several books. These days, Joel spends lots of time painting pictures in schools, hospitals, churches, and books. He lives in Holland, Michigan, with his cool wife, Kathy. Say "hi" to him at his site, www.joeltanis.com.

Judy Love grew up in an old house in the Massachusetts countryside. She lived with assorted farm animals including a rock-chasing dog, a dancing pig, and enough brothers and sisters for a baseball team! Judy has always wanted to be an artist and has illustrated more books than she cares to count, for both kids and adults—although she is not above painting on walls! Judy now lives in Belmont, Massachusetts, with two sons who are also great artists, and many smaller pets now. She feels lucky to have such a fun and exciting life (*really!*).

The *Could You?* spread, as it has come to be known, was created by a great many of the artists—Kim, Roby, Judy, Lena, Megan, Joel, and Kevin and Ryan, who also worked on the design of the spread for more than 50 hours! *Phew!* In it, you will find more than 45 compound words...some are easy, and some are tricky. Just flip the page for a complete list. If you find others we forgot about, send us an email: info@dannyandkim.com.

Meet the author and musicians!

Danny Adlerman is a children's author and musician with passion. Danny loves making great music with great friends. He has produced and recorded three CDs, *...and a Happy New Year*; *One Size Fits All*; and *Listen UP!*, with a whole lot of friends—most especially Jim and Kurt (*Hi Jim! Hi Kurt!*), and Pete and Rob (*Hey Pete! Yo Rob!*) He also loves writing books that make the whole world read. Danny has ten books published with more on the way. He was born and raised in New Jersey, where he still lives today with his beautiful wife and partner, Kimi, and their three most perfectest children ever.

Danny enjoys cooking, and he is not and especially good bowler, but hey—you can't have everything.

Jim Babjak began playing the guitar at the age of 12. His interest in music led him to become a founding member, songwriter, and lead guitarist of the internationally acclaimed rock group The Smithereens. The Smithereens have sold more than 4 million albums worldwide. The band's music can be heard in numerous movies and soundtracks, such as *Bull Durham*, *Backdraft*, *Time Cop*, *Boys Don't Cry*, and *Harold & Kumar Go to White Castle*. They have appeared on many television shows including *Saturday Night Live*, *The Tonight Show With Jay Leno*, and MTV's *Unplugged*. You can hear more of Jim's music for kids and their families on *One Size Fits All* and *Listen UP!*, which he recorded with Danny (*and Kurt! Hi Kurt!*). Learn more about Jim at www.jimbabjak.com.

How Much Wood Could a Woodchuck Chuck?

Words by Danny Adlerman / Music by Jim Babjak

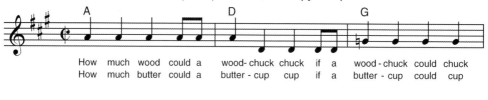

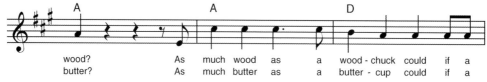

How much wood could a wood-chuck chuck if a wood-chuck could chuck
How much butter could a butter-cup cup if a butter-cup could cup

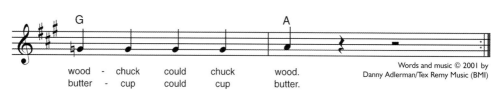

wood? As much wood as a wood-chuck could if a
butter? As much butter as a butter-cup could if a

wood - chuck could chuck wood.
butter - cup could cup butter.

3. How much fruit could a fruit bat bat if a fruit bat could bat fruit?
   As much fruit as a fruit bat could if a fruit bat could bat fruit.

4. How much straw could a strawberry bury if a strawberry could bury straw?
   As much straw as a strawberry could if a strawberry could bury straw.

5. How much man could a mandrill drill if a mandrill could drill man?
   As much man as a mandrill could if a mandrill could drill man.

6. How much night could a nightjar jar if a nightjar could jar night?
   As much night as a nightjar could if a nightjar could jar night.

7. How much sun could a sun bear bear if a sun bear could bear sun?
   As much sun as a sun bear could if a sun bear could bear sun.

8. How much fur could a fur seal seal if a fur seal could seal fur?
   As much fur as a fur seal could if a fur seal could seal fur.

9. How much chin could a chinchilla chill if a chinchilla could chill a chin?
   As much chin as a chinchilla could if a chinchilla could chill a chin.

10. How much ground could a groundhog hog if a groundhog could hog ground?
    As much ground as a groundhog could if a groundhog could hog ground.

11. How much chi could a cheetah tie if a cheetah could tai chi?
    As much chi as a cheetah could if a cheetah could tai chi.

12. How much could could a kudu you if a kudu could you could?
    As much could as a kudu could if a kudu could you could.
    Could you?

The *"Could you?"* spread has lots of pictures of the following compound words! How many did *you* find?

airplane, baseball, beehive, birdbath, birdhouse, bluebell, blueberries, bluebird, bowtie, bullfrog, bumblebee, butterfly, earring, eyeglasses, flagpole, football, grasshopper, hedgehog, hummingbird, jackrabbit, ladybug, lighthouse, mailbox, milkshake, necklace, ponytail (pigtail), rattlesnake, sailboat, sandpiper, seagull, seashell, sidewalk, spaceship, starfish, sundress, sunflower, surfboard, swordfish, watermelon

How about these?
afternoon, beach ball, crabgrass (or bluegrass), flip flop, outdoors, redhead, sand castle, seashore, skyline, summertime (or springtime), toejam (we know you can't see it, but trust us, it's there).

For those who think two-word compounds, like flip flop, is cheating: Did you know there are really three different types of compound words? They are:

1. Closed form: two words put together with no space between them, like most of what we used above;

2. Hyphenated form: more than one word separated by a hyphen but having a specific meaning like eight-year-old, brother-in-law, sergeant-at-arms, and six-pack;

3. Open form: two words that remain two separate words but still have a single meaning, like half moon, train station, and real estate.

We know because we looked it up!